SPARKS

The Birthday Party Mystery

Marion M. Markham

Illustrated by Pau Estrada

Houghton Mifflin Company

Boston 1989

Library of Congress Cataloging in Publication Data

Markham. Marion M.
    The birthday party mystery.

    Summary: Attending Debbie's birthday party at the
zoo, twin sleuths Kate and Mickey investigate the
mysterious disappearance of her presents.
    [1. Mystery and detective stories. 2. Zoos—
Fiction] I. Estrada, Pau, ill. II. Title.
PZ7.M33946Bi   1989   [Fic]   88-13465
ISBN: 0-395-49698-5

Printed in the United States of America

GO 10 9 8 7 6 5 4 3 2 1

Contents

1

Don't Talk to Strangers

Although it was Saturday morning, Mickey Dixon put on her new jeans and her best shirt. She and her twin sister, Kate, were going to Debbie Allen's birthday party at Animal Land.

"Take your jackets," Mrs. Dixon said. "The weather in April is so changeable."

Kate said, "It's a scientific fact —"

Mickey interrupted her sister. "No scientific facts, please. We'll be late for the party."

Kate wanted to be a scientist, and she was always telling her sister scientific facts. Mickey thought science was boring, except when it helped to solve mysteries. Mickey wanted to be a detective.

"Remember," Mrs. Dixon said as they left. "Don't talk to strangers." That was something *she* was always telling them.

"We won't," Mickey and Kate said together.

Outside, the morning was warm and the sky was a lovely deep blue. It was a perfect day for a birthday party.

Animal Land was on Bay Street, north of the city park. It had a small zoo as well as a merry-go-round and other rides for children. Debbie and her mother were waiting outside the Giraffe Gate for them. When all the guests were there, they entered under the arched necks of two wooden giraffes.

The ticket taker glared at them suspiciously as they filed through the turnstile. Mrs. Allen was last in line, and the man told her to check in with a security guard. The guard stood just inside the gate, looking very serious. He waved his hands as he spoke to Debbie's mother, and she bobbed her head.

"What was that all about?" asked Mickey.

Mrs. Allen said, "He told me that I am responsible for all of you."

"Responsible?" asked Billy Wade.

Debbie said, "He means Mother is in trouble if *you* get in trouble." She looked him right in the eye as she said it. Billy Wade was the biggest troublemaker in the fourth grade.

Mrs. Allen led them to an area where four old circus wagons were lined up. But instead of real animals, canvas awnings with animals painted on them were hung behind the bars. Debbie opened the door to the red lion wagon. Inside, balloons and streamers fluttered from the ceiling, and a table had been set for the party. The pink-and-white cake in the center of the table said HAPPY BIRTHDAY, DEBBIE.

Mrs. Allen took the presents the boys and girls had brought and set them on the table. Debbie gave each of them a book of tickets.

Her mother explained, "You can use these for rides or to buy souvenirs. But be back for lunch at eleven-thirty. And remember. *Don't get into trouble!*"

2

The Gray Man

Outside, the children scattered in different directions for their favorite rides.

Mickey noticed that a guard followed two of the boys toward the prairie animal exhibit.

"I'm going to see the monkeys first," said Kate. Mickey wanted to ride the little train that ran around the park. But when Billy Wade said that he was going there, she decided to stay with her sister.

The zoo was not large, but it was a favorite place for Springvale children on a warm Saturday. Mothers and fathers pushed empty strollers while tots cuddled baby rabbits on their laps or let fawns lick their hands.

When Mickey and Kate saw a camel with sagging humps, Kate said, "A camel's humps are made of fat. This one probably used most of his fat keeping warm over the winter."

"I know." Mickey mimicked Kate's voice. "It's a scientific fact that camels live in hot deserts."

Kate shook her head. "Deserts are dry, but they aren't necessarily hot," she said. "The Gobi Desert is very cold."

To change the subject, Mickey asked, "Do you notice that strange man watching us?" Kate turned.

The man certainly *was* strange. Everything about him was gray: his hair, his eyes, his wrinkled clothing, and even his skin.

He smiled at them and said, "Hello, girls. Are you here all alone?"

"No," said Mickey quickly. "Our mother is buying popcorn." She grabbed Kate's hand and pulled her toward the popcorn cart.

Because they were looking back to see if the man was going to follow them, the twins didn't notice a young woman until they bumped into her. She had curly red hair, and her eyes were the color of purple violets.

"Whoa," she said, and her voice was sharp. "Where are you going in such a hurry?"

Mickey said, "We were running away from the gray man."

Kate said, "He tried to talk to us."

The woman smiled, a friendly smile that made her look younger. "Smart girls," she said. "Never talk to strangers. It's dangerous." She leaned down and whispered. "It's really not good for you to be here in Animal Land."

Mickey said, "You mean the rides aren't safe?"

"I mean some very strange things have been happening here lately."

"What sort of things?" Mickey asked.

"Very mysterious things," the woman said softly. "You shouldn't come here anymore. It's not a safe place for children to be alone."

"We're not alone," said Kate. "There are nine of us, ten counting Debbie, and we're here for her birthday party."

"Where is the birthday party?" the woman asked.

Mickey pointed toward the group of circus wagons. "In the red wagon — the one with the lion."

"I guess you're all right then," the woman said. "Have you ridden the train yet?"

"No," said Mickey. "I was going to do that first. Then Billy Wade said that was where *he* was going. No one wants to ride with Billy Wade."

The woman laughed. "I understand. I had a Billy Wade in my class when I was about your age."

"You did?" said Kate. "What a strange coincidence."

"I don't mean his name was Billy Wade. Actually, I think he was called Bobby. But he was always pulling the girls' hair or sticking his foot out to trip someone."

Kate said, "That's Billy Wade, all right."

They heard the toot, toot of the Animal Land Express. "You'd better run if you want to catch the train," the woman said. "And be careful!"

The train's brakes hissed, and the open cars coasted to a stop.

"Climb aboard, girls," called the engineer as he took their tickets. He pulled a chain, and the whistle tooted again.

Each car of the train was supposed to be a different animal. The engine was a grinning shark with a big, toothy smile. Kate and Mickey climbed into the black-and-white-striped zebra.

As the train started, they waved to the woman. But her back was toward them, and she didn't notice.

The gray man waved at them, though.

Kate pulled her arm down quickly. She didn't want the man to think she was waving at him.

"Gosh, he was scary," said Mickey. "Lucky for us that woman was there."

Kate said, "We ought to tell someone about him."

3

More Trouble

The tracks wound past a barnyard of farm animals and then curved around a pond of ducks and geese. In a very small grove of trees, a little boy was petting a baby deer.

The engineer tooted the whistle, and the train stopped in front of the walrus tank.

"Look," said Kate. "There's Mrs. Allen with some of the kids." The twins jumped off.

"Hello, girls," Mrs. Allen said. "You came to see them feed the walrus, too."

Kate said, "In the ocean, a walrus digs for clams with its tusks."

"Who cares?" Mickey said. She told Mrs. Allen about the strange gray man. "He scared us and we ran away from him. But a woman was there and she warned us to be careful. And then we got away on the train." She said it without stopping for breath.

"Oh, dear," Mrs. Allen said. "The guard told me to watch all of you, but I thought he meant so that you wouldn't *cause* trouble."

Kate said, "We're all right. Mickey likes to make everything into a mystery."

Mickey was about to say that she didn't make *everything* into a mystery, only those things that were really mysterious. But when she saw how pale Mrs. Allen was, she said, "We weren't really in any danger."

"Still, I think we'd all better get back to the lion wagon," said Mrs. Allen, motioning everyone onto the waiting train.

When the train stopped near the circus wagons, Debbie was the first one off. She raced to the lion wagon and opened the door. Then she screamed.

"Debbie, what is it?" her mother asked.

"My birthday presents are gone!"

4

The Clown Who Liked Raisins

The other boys and girls pushed past Debbie into the lion wagon. Sure enough, the packages were gone and Debbie's birthday cake had been smashed into a gooey glob of pink frosting and crumbs.

Debbie began crying. "Everything's spoiled," she said between sobs.

Mrs. Allen hugged her. "It's all right. We can buy another birthday cake."

"But I want my presents," Debbie wailed. Her sobs grew louder and louder.

A short, fat clown with a big red smile painted on his face rapped on the open door.

"What's the matter?" he said.

"Someone stole my birthday presents," Debbie wailed. "And squished my birthday cake."

"Bless my sneakers," the clown said.

Kate giggled. "Bless my sneakers?" she whispered to Mickey.

The clown reached into his costume and took out a handful of raisins.

"Bless my sneakers," he repeated and popped the raisins into his mouth.

The twins knew only one person in Springvale who was always eating raisins.

Mickey said, "Officer Huggins!"

The clown said, "Hello, girls. Officer Finney told me you were here."

Mickey said, "We never saw Officer Finney."

"He said you did. You even waved to him from the train."

"The gray man," Kate and Mickey said together.

Kate said, "We didn't recognize him."

"What a neat disguise," Mickey said. "He'll have to show me how he did it."

"He really fooled you? He'll be so happy. He wasn't sure the disguise worked. Mine is easier, because I can paint my face."

"And go around saying, 'Bless my sneakers'?" Kate asked.

Officer Huggins's painted red cheeks turned even redder. "I'm supposed to be funny," he said. "That usually gets a laugh from the boys and girls." He looked at Debbie, who was still sniffling. "It doesn't always work, though."

"There's nothing funny about this," Mrs. Allen said. "If you're really a police officer" — her voice sounded doubtful — "I demand that you find the thief and make him return the packages."

Mickey said, "He *is* a policeman. We've worked together on a couple of cases."

"I'd better report this to Mr. Ferris, the owner," Officer Huggins said. He took a walkie-talkie from a pocket in his baggy costume and spoke into it.

"Spy One to Ferris. Spy One to Ferris." He flipped a switch and waited. When there was no response he called again, "Spy One to Ferris. Do you read me? Come in, Ferris."

A gravelly voice answered, "Don't be so durned impatient. I heard you all right, but I had a doughnut in my mouth. Over."

Officer Huggins said, "Spy One reporting a robbery. Birthday presents stolen from the lion wagon, and a birthday cake destroyed. Over."

"Oh dear, oh dear," said the gravel-voiced Ferris. This time he didn't say "over," but they could tell from the sound that he had flipped the walkie-talkie switch.

"Close the front gate," Officer Huggins ordered. "Don't let anyone out. Over."

"I can't do that," Ferris called. "People will get angry. They'll never come back. Without people, Animal Land will have to close. Oh dear." The walkie-talkie went dead, then crackled on again as the man remembered to add, "Over."

Officer Huggins thought for a moment. Then he said, "Stop anyone who tries to leave with" — he raised a finger and counted the guests — "nine birthday presents. Over and out."

"No one would be dumb enough to walk out with packages wrapped in birthday paper," Mickey whispered to Kate. "He would rip them open and hide what he could in his pockets. Or toss them over the fence and pick them up later."

As Officer Huggins tucked the walkie-talkie back into his pocket, Mrs. Allen said, "Mr. Ferris absolutely assured me that Animal Land would be a safe place to hold a birthday party."

"So it has been — for the visitors," said Officer Huggins.

"What do you mean?" asked Mickey.

"Someone has been feeding the animals."

Mrs. Allen said, "I know there are signs all around saying not to feed them. But I wouldn't think it was the job of the police to enforce the rule. You might better spend your time watching for people who steal birthday presents."

"When someone is deliberately feeding the animals something to make them sick, it becomes police business," Officer Huggins said.

"Oh," said Mrs. Allen.

Mickey said, "How terrible."

"There have been other things, too," Officer Huggins said. "Black paint sprayed on the Animal Land Express. A water fountain that was deliberately broken."

"Who's doing it?" asked one of the boys.

"We don't know," said Officer Huggins. "Nothing has happened since Officer Finney and I came on the case."

Kate, who had been bobbing back and forth between her right foot and her left, finally got to ask the question she had been wondering about. "Officer Finney has brown eyes. How did he make them gray?" she said.

"Contact lenses," said Officer Huggins.

Mickey said, "If you had read *The Handbook of One Thousand Disguises* instead of all that science, you'd know."

Debbie said, "What about my birthday presents?"

5

Where's Billy Wade?

"As I see it, we have two choices," Officer Huggins said. "We find out who took the presents and make him tell us where they are. Or we search for the presents and hope that they will give us a clue to the identity of the thief."

"I know who took the presents," said Debbie. "Billy Wade. He's mean enough to wreck anyone's party. I didn't want to invite him in the first place."

Her mother said, "William's mother is my closest friend, and he's been to every one of your birthday parties."

"And he's spoiled half of them. Remember last year? He spilled pepper in the fruit punch."

"That was an accident," her mother said. "He didn't know the top was loose when he tossed the pepper shaker in the air."

"He probably loosened it himself," Debbie said.

Officer Huggins said, "Where is this Billy Wade?"

One of the boys said, "He was going to ride the train."

"Then let's wait for him at the train stop," said Officer Huggins.

Kate said, "Hold on. How many trains are there?"

"Two," said Officer Huggins.

"He wasn't on the train we took to get back here. And Mickey and I didn't see him on the one before that either."

"Of course not," said Mickey. "If he was still on the train, he couldn't have sneaked back here to wreck the party."

Officer Huggins said, "You're right. We'd better organize a search."

Debbie said, "To look for my presents?"

"To look for Billy *and* your presents," said Officer Huggins.

"Whoopee," said one of the boys.

Mrs. Allen said, "You're all staying right here. I'm responsible for your safety, and I won't have you wandering around when there's a criminal on the loose."

Kate said, "I don't think Billy is really a criminal."

"He stole my presents," said Debbie.

Her mother said, "We don't know that."

Mickey, who didn't intend to be left behind when a mystery was going on, said, "We could search and still be safe."

"How?" said Mrs. Allen.

"Am I right that the train goes all around Animal Land?"

Officer Huggins nodded.

"If we spread out in a line on either side of the track, we could make a wide sweep around the entire park," Mickey explained. "And if we leave fifteen or twenty feet between us, we can keep sight of each other and still look for Billy and the presents."

Officer Huggins thought it was a good idea, but Mrs. Allen looked doubtful.

Then Debbie said, "It's *my* birthday, and I want to look for *my* presents," and so her mother finally agreed.

Outside, clouds had covered the sun, and the breeze off the lake had gotten stronger.

"Put on your jacket," Kate said to Mickey. She knew that when her twin was looking for clues, she wouldn't notice a blizzard if it wasn't part of the mystery.

Mrs. Allen insisted that she wanted to be in the middle so that she could keep track of both sides of the search party. Officer Huggins took the outside edge along the fence. Mickey put Kate and herself on the inner edge of the line.

"There are more places to hide in the middle of Animal Land," she told Kate.

"What will we do when we come to a pond?"
Debbie said.

"Go around it, of course," said Mickey. "We
don't always have to be *exactly* twenty feet apart as
long as we can still see each other."

They didn't need to go around the pond,
though, because it was there that they found Billy.
He was struggling to get away from the gray man.
The disguise was so good that, for a second, Kate
forgot that the gray man was really Officer Finney.

Officer Huggins trotted in from the end of the
line.

"Billy Wade?" His voice was very stern.

Billy called, "Mrs. Allen. Help me."

Mrs. Allen said, "Let go of that boy."

Officer Finney said, "He was feeding jellybeans
to the geese. One goose almost choked to death."

"I hope it was the one who tried to bite me,"
one of the girls whispered loudly.

"What did you do with the birthday presents?" Officer Huggins asked.

"Birthday presents?" Billy yelled. "I don't know anything about any birthday presents, and anyone who says I do is a liar."

Debbie said. "*My* birthday presents. They're gone. And this is the last time you're invited to my party."

"I didn't take your dumb presents," Billy said. "And I don't want to go to your dumb parties, only my mother makes me." He tried to sound tough, but he looked frightened.

6

Where Did the Jellybeans Come From?

Mickey had been thinking about jellybeans, spray paint, and mashed cake. She said, "I think there's more going on than jellybeans or just taking Debbie's presents."

"*Just* taking my birthday presents." Debbie sounded indignant.

Her mother said, "Debbie, stop whining."

"What do you mean?" asked Officer Huggins.

Mrs. Allen said, "I mean that I've heard about nothing but her birthday presents for the last month, and I'm tired of it."

"I was asking what Mickey meant," said Officer Huggins.

"Oh," said Mrs. Allen. She sighed and shook her head.

Mickey said, "It's a simple deduction. Someone sprays paint on the trains and gives the animals something to make them sick. Then the police begin to watch, so he stops. He must *know* the police are watching."

"Which means their disguises didn't fool him," Kate said.

Officer Finney said, "I fooled you."

"With *this* disguise," said Mickey. "But maybe one of your other disguises wasn't as good."

Officer Huggins looked confused. "What other disguises?"

Kate said, "You mean you've worn the same disguise every day?"

"Sure," said Officer Finney.

"Even I know that a gray man loitering around Animal Land all the time would be pretty notice-able after a few days."

Officer Finney said, "I should have thought of that. But it was such a *good* disguise."

"So it was," Mickey said. "But your disguise might not have mattered. It could be an inside job — an unhappy employee who wants to get even with Mr. Ferris. He would know that Mr. Ferris called the police. So he made trouble only in

places where the police weren't watching."

Officer Finney said, "Like the goose pond and the circus wagons."

"Then we should try to find out who has a grudge against Mr. Ferris," said Officer Huggins.

Mickey said, "We should find out where Billy got the jellybeans."

Officer Huggins asked, "Why?"

"Billy Wade is a troublemaker. But I don't think he would have thought of giving jellybeans to geese."

Billy had been listening quietly to the conversation — probably the first time in his life he wasn't trying to attract attention, Kate thought.

Now he shouted, "I didn't."

Mrs. Allen said, "You see. He didn't. It was that awful man who talked to the Dixon twins."

Officer Finney said, "I'm the man who talked to the Dixon twins. I'm also a policeman."

Mrs. Allen wrinkled her forehead. She looked puzzled.

Debbie said, "And you think Billy wasn't the one who took my presents?"

"I think that only one person is causing all the trouble," said Mickey.

Officer Huggins turned to Billy. "Where did you get the jellybeans?"

Billy's voice cracked as he tried to talk. He cleared his throat and started again.

"A woman gave them to me. She told me they packed them especially for feeding the geese." As he spoke, Billy searched his pockets. "See. Here's the bag they came in," he said triumphantly.

The bag was bright red, and someone had printed GOOSE FOOD on it with letters from a rubber stamp set.

Kate asked, "What did the woman look like?"

"She was just an ordinary woman with gray hair. Maybe the boy at the refreshment stand got a better look."

"At the refreshment stand?" Mickey asked.

"Where she bought the jellybeans she gave me to feed the geese."

Kate said, "Didn't you think it was odd that a strange woman would buy jellybeans for you?"

"I never think," said Billy.

Officer Finney said, "*I* think we'd better talk to the boy at the refreshment stand."

Everyone headed that way except Mrs. Allen, who seemed even more puzzled.

The young man behind the counter was wearing a white paper cap that said RICK on the band. Because he was reading a book, he didn't notice them until Mickey whistled sharply.

He grinned and said, "May I help you?"

Officer Finney handed the red bag to him. "Did you sell this?" he asked.

"Of course not. The only thing we've ever sold for the animals is cracked corn." He showed them a small bag, and they could see the corn through the plastic. "Only, we stopped when all the trouble started."

Mickey asked, "Did anyone buy jellybeans this morning?"

Rick said, "Jellybeans aren't popular in the morning. Too sweet."

Officer Huggins said, "You ought to sell raisins. They're very good in the morning — or anytime."

As if he hadn't been interrupted, Rick continued. "That's why I remember the gray-haired woman. She bought two bags of jellybeans."

"Two bags?" said Officer Finney.

"Not together. She bought one bag and then came back a half hour later for the second one."

"Did you see her eat them?" Kate asked.

"I just take their money," Rick said. "What they do with them is their business."

"Even if they feed jellybeans to the geese?" Officer Finney said sternly.

"Hey, I would have noticed that." Then he added, "Is that what she did?"

Billy asked, "Why would the woman go back to the refreshment stand twice?"

"To make you believe the stand was selling bags of jellybeans for the geese."

"Huh?"

Mickey said, "After she bought the first bag of jellybeans, she had to go someplace where no one could see her put them into the red bag marked GOOSE FOOD."

"I still don't see why she bought a second bag."

Mickey explained, "Because she wanted you to *see her buy jellybeans*."

"But why?" asked Billy.

Kate said, "So you wouldn't get suspicious."

"I wouldn't have been suspicious of a bag marked GOOSE FOOD," Billy said.

Mickey said, "She didn't know that . . ." She almost said, "that you're dumb." But she didn't, because Billy wasn't dumb. When he used his brain, he was the smartest boy in their class. Only most of the time he didn't use his brain. He just acted and then got into trouble.

Mickey asked Rick, "Did you recognize the woman? Maybe someone who worked here at one time?"

"Naw, I didn't know her. And I would have remembered, because she had gray hair, but her face wasn't old. I mean, she looked about twenty years old."

"It's too bad you don't have your fingerprint kit with you," Kate said to Mickey. "You could dust the bag for prints and find out who she is."

"Not after everyone has handled it," Mickey said. "Besides, I'd need her prints to compare them with."

Debbie said, "What about my birthday presents?"

Officer Huggins took out his walkie-talkie. "I'll alert Mr. Ferris so the security guards can watch for a young woman with prematurely gray hair."

"And violet eyes," Rick said.

"Violet eyes!" said Kate. "Are you sure?"

"Positive. I've never seen eyes that color before."

"Then it has to be the same woman we saw," Mickey said. "Only she was wearing a gray wig over her red hair."

"It's a good thing *she* didn't read about contact lenses in *The Handbook of One Thousand Disguises*," Kate said.

Mickey said, "Let's see if Mr. Ferris knows a girl with violet eyes and red hair."

"My thought exactly," said Officer Finney.

They heard a toot, toot.

"There's the train," he said. "If we hurry we can catch it."

Officer Huggins was already dashing toward the tracks. Kate was surprised that the fat policeman could move so fast.

"Toot, toot," went the train whistle.

"All aboard," called the engineer.

"Hey, wait for us," Billy yelled.

When she saw everyone running, Mrs. Allen dashed for the train, too.

The Animal Land office was near the front gate. As they entered, Mickey and Kate saw Mr. Ferris signing something. And the girl with the violet eyes was sitting across the desk from him. But now she had dark hair, so she must have worn a red wig, too.

"That's her," said Billy. "The lady who gave me jellybeans to feed the geese. Her hair is different, but I recognize her face."

"What's this all about?" Mr. Ferris asked.

Debbie pointed to the girl. "She stole my birthday presents."

"I did not."

Mickey said, "She's the one who's been causing all the trouble in Animal Land."

Mr. Ferris said, "Impossible. Miss Williams is the granddaughter of the man who started Animal Land. And when all the bad things started, she offered me fifty acres outside of town for a new park."

Kate said, "What's going to happen to this land?"

Miss Williams said, "I'll sell it to some people who want to build condominiums along the lake."

"Aha," said Mickey. "The motive for the crime. You wanted this property, and the only way you could get it was to convince Mr. Ferris to move Animal Land."

The girl smiled, but it wasn't the friendly smile they had seen before. "My grandfather was an idiot. When he retired from Animal Land, he gave Ferris a ninety-nine-year lease. This property belongs to me, but I couldn't sell it because of a stupid piece of paper." She paused. "They'll pay me three million dollars. Surely you understand that's more important than a recreation park."

Mrs. Allen said, "Not to the boys and girls of Springvale."

"It doesn't matter," Miss Williams said. *"Now."*

Mr. Ferris said, "I just signed a contract trading this land for her farm outside of town."

Mickey said, "That contract isn't valid. You were tricked into signing it." She looked at Officer Finney for support.

"Coercion," he said. "It means pressuring someone to do something he doesn't want to do, and it's illegal."

Miss Williams said. "You can't prove I did anything wrong."

Billy said, "I know you gave me the jellybeans that choked the goose."

Kate said, "You stole Debbie's birthday presents."

"That's right," said Officer Huggins.

"I didn't steal them. I simply moved them to the tiger wagon."

Debbie said, "You smashed my birthday cake."

Miss Williams said, "I don't think the town council has ever passed a law protecting birthday cakes. Now, if you'll excuse me." She reached across the desk for the contract. But Billy got it first.

"Give me that," Miss Williams said. She tried to grab Billy, but he ducked away from her.

"Sure," said Billy. He tore the contract in half.

Miss Williams tried to catch him, but Billy was faster and he avoided her easily as she chased him around the office.

"Stop him," she screamed.

But everyone just watched while he tore the contract into bits of paper and dropped them on the floor. Miss Williams kneeled down and tried to

put them together. Tears fell from her violet eyes, turning Mr. Ferris's signature into a blurry smudge. She kept repeating, "Three million dollars."

Debbie said, "Don't tell me you never think, Billy Wade." Billy looked embarrassed.

Officer Finney helped Miss Williams up. "Do you want to press charges against her?" he asked Mr. Ferris.

"Not if she promises to stay away from Animal Land."

She glared at him but didn't say anything.

Officer Huggins said, "If you ever come back here, we'll arrest you for disturbing the peace."

"And harassment," Officer Finney added.

Mickey said, "Don't forget coercion."

"I won't be back," Miss Williams said and slammed out the door.

"Now can we find my birthday presents?" Debbie asked.

"I'm sorry about your cake," Mr. Ferris said.

Debbie said, "I guess it was really a good thing. I mean, if she hadn't spoiled my party, the Dixon twins wouldn't have gotten involved, and Animal Land would have moved away."

Mickey said, "I just thought of something."

"What?" said Officer Finney.

"We were afraid of you, but it was Miss Williams who was the one we should have been worried about."

"Bad people don't always look like bad people," he said.

Kate said, "Miss Williams didn't." She grinned at her sister. "You even told her where the party was."

"I guess I did," Mickey said.

"If we *don't find my presents now*, there isn't going to be a party," said Debbie.

They did find them in the tiger wagon, and even without a cake, the twins thought it was the best birthday party ever. Mrs. Allen had brought lemonade, potato chips, and lots of sandwiches — ham, turkey, peanut butter and jelly, and egg salad. And they all got fancy hats and paper horns that unwound as they blew into them.

Mr. Ferris brought ice cream bars and stayed to have a glass of lemonade and a turkey sandwich.

Between bites, he told Billy, "You sure took care of that contract."

"Practice. I've been grabbing things away from girls for years," Billy said and snatched Debbie's hat from her head.

"Billy!" Mrs. Allen said. "You will never again be invited to one of Debbie's parties."

Debbie said, "It's my party, and I can invite who I want."

Then Mr. Ferris said to the twins, "Officer

Huggins told me you girls were the ones who organized the search. And recognized the clue of the violet eyes."

Mickey said, "It was just a matter of asking the right questions. And making a simple deduction."

Kate smiled at her twin. Maybe Mickey *would* be a detective when she got older. Mickey Dixon, private eye. It sounded almost as good as Kate Dixon, scientist.